Crunchy and Good with Ketchup

Fantasy and Role-Playing Jokes

TH Leatherman

Crunchy and Good with Ketchup by TH Leatherman

Published by Fivefold Publishing LLC, PO Box 586, Firestone, CO 80520.

ISBN: 978-1-7353990-9-6

ACKNOWLEDGEMENTS

A thank you to my D&D players. We've been playing together for six years, and it's been a blast. For every dungeon we've delved or kingdom we've saved, you've been there rolling dice and kicking kobolds with the best of them. Through it all you laughed at my jokes, groaned at my puns, and solved my puzzles and I cherish every moment that we spent together. Some of you have moved on to run your own campaigns and I look forward to spending as many fun years in your worlds as you spent in mine.

Thanks also to Drake and Ashton Corriveau, Katrina Watts, Noah and Jack Watts, Caleb, Will, Levy Mays, Jake Frank, Alex Miller, Matt, Kristina, Stephanie, CJ, Walker, Jim Bartlemay, Brian Hirsch, Kat Kane, Kerry Cox, Lise Harwick, Robert Lizak, Paul Dubro, Paul Clark, Hayden Snow, and way too many more people to name here. Playing with you over the years has been fun. Your support has been invaluable. I'll gladly sit down at a table with you anytime.

FORWARD

(Meddle not in the affairs of dragons, for you are crunchy and good with ketchup!)

This is book is for all of the players and game masters who have played fantasy role-playing games over the past forty plus years. I am that one friend who will always seize the opportunity to run a D&D game. A Carpe D.M. if you will. I've made some great dungeons, told even greater stories, and thrown more challenges and monsters at my players than I can possibly count. And I've told a lot of role-playing related dad jokes. Now that my son has graciously decided to follow in my footsteps, I sometimes I even get to play. When I do, I do it for... the experience.

And now I am passing all my corny role-playing dad jokes on to you. When you gather your friends and family to take on the evil wizard that's raising horses from the dead (a neigh-cromancer) or assault the castle on top of an enormous turtle (a tort-tress), I hope you'll think of this book. I've found that jokes, puns, and humor add to the enjoyment of an adventure and have kept players coming back to the table week after week. Now you can bring some laughs and groans to your game as well. Hopefully they'll make your next campaign a critical success!

CONTENTS

(How do you tell a treasure chest from a mimic? It's easy. Look inside.)

1 GENERAL ROLEPLAYING MADNESS

People love hit points. They're the life of the party.

Campaigns in the frozen north can lead to a total party chill.

What's a party's greatest obstacle? Scheduling a session.

Where do die 10s come from? The Percent Isles.

I grabbed some popcorn as the bowl went by. It was a Snack of Opportunity.

I have an enchanted mattress. It brings magic to the bedroom.

Dungeon masters are always in great shape. They do a lots of running.

The weather is getting worse. Instead of raining cats and dogs, it's hailing adventurers.

Vegan adventurers never meat in a tavern.

There's a magic portal somewhere in the dungeon. The party is looking into it.

I took my weapon to the wedding. It was my +1.

You can't put a king at the beginning of a sentence. They aren't subjects.

The new ogre gladiator tears his opponents apart, but my friend said not to go see him. It was a rip off.

We've nicknamed our tank Life Alert. He's fallen and can't get up.

Why is the evil artifact humming? Because it doesn't know the words.

D&D players are good people. They have character.

My friends keep sending me interlocking rings by post. It's chain mail.

That cursed tome must be really interesting. The Wizard can't put it down.

I gave my players copies of Lord of the Rings. As a Tolkien of my appreciation.

I dreamt I was in The Lord of the Rings. My wife says I was Tolkien in my sleep.

My life is like a fairy tale, Grimm.

The fairy tale character that knows the most jokes. Ra-pun-zel.

You know your magic sword is blunt when it starts criticizing your swordsmanship.

Ethereal Rocks give you a choice of Ether Ore.

So you're playing D&D with your friends? That sounds dicey.

The greatest obstacle my player face? Scheduling a game.

I accidentally knocked over my magic cream, but I don't cry over spelled milk.

Did you know Frodo is fifty years old in the books? That's how he survived Mount Doom. Old Hobbits die hard.

I asked the lion what he was doing in my wardrobe. He said Narnia business.

Hobbits save food by covering it in Sauron wrap.

I searched for "missing medieval servant", and it came back "page not found".

I started walking around with no shoes, and it sort of became a Hobbit.

Anyone who doesn't like The Lord of the Rings doesn't know what they're Tolkien about.

The evil queen turned out to be a gnoll. We ended her reign of terrier.

There's a science to granting wishes. Genie-ology.

My favorite tea is natural twen-tea.

2 CHARACTER CLASSES

BARBARIAN

Our Barbarian used to work as an executioner. He wanted to get a head in life.

High Damage is popular with Barbarians. It's all the Rage.

Our Barbarian never goes anywhere without his favorite weapon. It's a Great Axe.

If the Barbarian has twenty gold, and the Rogue steals half of it, how much did the Rogue take? 1d12 slashing.

My weapon came from a kingdom far to the east. That's why it has that foreign axe scent.

I have a magic axe that sometimes gives compliments. It's a random axe of kindness.

BARD

Never trust a bard, they're often seen with lyres.

An unemployed jester is nobody's fool.

Our bard has a ghost lute. It plays haunting melodies.

Musicians should always warm up before a performance to avoid minstrel cramps.

Our party musician specializes in Freedom of Movement spells. He's a No Holds Bard.

Our Bard is cursed with silence, but we still keep him in the party. A mime is a terrible thing to waste.

Bards go on adventures for the lute.

CLERIC

My Tempest Cleric has special under garments. Thunderwear!

Our cleric is sick and can't cast Create Water. I told him to get *well* soon!

Our cleric has a secondary profession as a cobbler. He wants to save soles.

The best place to hit a Cleric is right in the temple.

Clerics in training make their own sermons. It's a write of passage.

Our War Cleric accidentally attacked the NPC. It was a clerical error.

DRUID

Our Druid was arrested for summoning crows. It was an attempted murder.

Lazy Druids do the Bear minimum.

Druids don't move very fast, they're stuck in Neutral.

Druids change the color of their leathers with a dyer wolf.

Our Druid stopped combat with an Entangle spell. It was de-vine intervention.

The Druid was kicked out of the forest for arranging squirrels by height. They don't like it when other people critter size them.

6 FIGHTERS, PALADINS, AND KNIGHTS

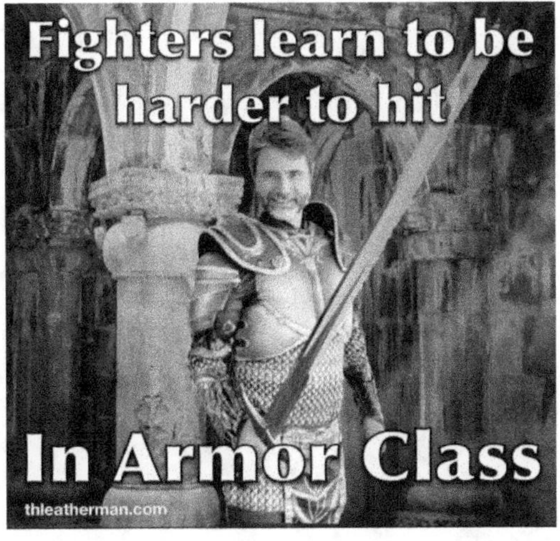

Being the most popular squire in the castle, I worked most Knights.

Fighters combat the heat by turning up the AC.

It's called the dark ages because there were a lot of Knights.

Playing a Monk is easy, just roll with the punches.

The Paladin's horse was stolen. He's searching for clues, but so far he has nothing to go on.

Paladins wear chain mail because it's holey armor.

Justice is best served cold, because otherwise it's just water.

I went to Knight school to learn how to slay dragons.

The kingdom is having Knight try-outs promptly at 3 on Tuesday. Be there or be Squire.

Why do Paladins require 8 hours of rest to regain spells? Because they need a good Knight's sleep.

It takes two Paladins to light a candle. One to light it and another to, “uphold the light.”

MONKS

A Monk's favorite drink is punch!

Monk versus archers, flurry of bows

Always let the Monk buy coffee for the party. They'll have a punch card.

If you can't get into your house, find a Monk. They always have a ki.

RANGER

Broken arrows are pointless

Where do Rangers keep their arrows? In the monsters.

Rangers use arrows to get their point across.

Whenever the party goes into combat, the Ranger quivers with joy.

Rangers eat pepper so they'll always habanero.

I know it's a long shot, but does anyone have a compound bow I could borrow?

When the monster broke our Ranger's bow, he became de-ranged.

ROGUE

You can't hear gnome rogues. The "G" is silent.

Why did the Ranger/Rogue keep getting into fights? He was duel classed.

I know a Rogue who's also an acupuncturist. He gives a good Backstab.

Rogues are easily offended. They're always taking things literally.

Rogues always steal from Bards because they have the best lute.

Always let Rogue get the party's provisions. They're great at Slight of Ham.

A Rogue's favorite metal is Steel. Their least favorite is Copper.

Sensitive Rogues take everything personally.

I saw an elf rogue pickpocket a dwarf. How could he stoop so low?

Rogues have clean consciouses. It’s never been used.

A rogue’s favorite footwear? Sneakers.

Never raise your hand to a rogue. It leaves your coin purse unprotected.

My rogue has demonic parentage. A theif-ling.

WIZARDS

Wizards often have great staff

Our wizard claims he can walk through walls, but I think he's going through a phase.

The difference between wizards and sorcerers is Class.

The wizard made it to town first. He really booked it.

Wizards proof their magic with a spell checker.

What do you get when you cross the Wizard and the Rogue? Roll initiative.

Wizards like Fireball because it's a well-rounded spell.

Necromancers aren't all bad. They just want to raise a family in peace.

Wizard Sous Chefs are Saucerors.

The village wizard has fallen on hard times. He had to let his staff go.

I know a wizard that specializes in eyesight spells. He's an Opti-Mystic.

I'm an Ice Wizard. A Blizzard.

Our wizard likes fireball. Consider this your Burn Notice.

The Evil Wizard offered me anything from his chest to just walk away. I screamed, "The only thing I want from your chest is your heart!" So, our first date is next week...

Harry Potter puns are sneaky. You never know when they'll Slytherin.

As a wizard, I enjoy turning things into glass. Just to make things clear.

My wizard friend uses Levitate to hold up his camera. It's for Spell-fies.

The divination college at the wizard academy has been closed because of unforeseen circumstances.

I’m thinking about playing a wizard. I'll try that for a spell.

I knew a magician who lost his magic. Now we call him Ian.

I showed a mime a magic trick. He was speechless.

Have you read the book on teleportation? It will take you places.

I raise horses from the dead. I’m a neighcromancer.

A Wizard Tournament is also known as a Spelling B.

My friend is playing a gnome Divination Wizard. He’s a small medium at large.

Necromancy wizards are swoll! It’s all the deadlifting.

How do enchanters make magical sticks? Wand you like to know.

3 SPELLS

The best spell when you see someone who needs a hug? Hold Person.

My Invisibility spell didn't expire. I went to a cleric for help, but they couldn't see me.

It's not ice cream, it's my Cone of Cold.

The longest lasting first level spell is Friends. It lasted ten seasons.

When I want some alone time, I drink Invisibili-tea.

Whenever I go someplace new, I cast Find Familiar to get to know the place.

I was startled when the wizard grabbed me. It was a Shocking Grasp.

I never worry about sickly yellow torches. I can Cure Light.

Our wizard forgot to prepare Light. It was a dark time.

I accidentally cast Silence on my wife. She isn't speaking to me.

Don't cast unlocking spells on every door you see. Don't Knock it, 'til you try it.

Don't get disheartened when you know what your enemies are up to. It's nothing to Scry about.

If you use Ray of Frost out of combat, you'll only get cold shoulders.

The enemy wizard cast Web. It was a sticky situation.

Casting Levitate isn't always a good thing. It has its ups and downs.

4 CHARACTER RACES

DWARVES

Dwarves get new hammers at the maul

Dwarves' favorite music? Rock Music.

For dwarves, if it doesn't matter, they don't mine.

When a dwarf is in the party, always make sure you have extra coin for bills. They're always a little short.

Who would stoop so low as to steal from a dwarf?

I asked the Gloomstalker how to tell the difference between a cave system and a mine. He said if it's dwarves, it's mine.

6 out of 7 dwarves aren't Happy.

There are no dwarven lawyers. They can't pass the Bar.

How do you get the dwarves to the roof? Tell them drinks are on the house.

Dwarves hunt dragons in the morning because they know the early beard catches the wyrm.

The wizard said, "Isn't it strange how little people change?" That got me to thinking. Do dwarves put on clothes differently than the rest of us?

A genie appeared and granted me one wish. I said I wanted to be happy. Now I live in a forest cottage with 6 other dwarfs.

Our dwarf pulled a muscle while digging for gold. No worries though, it's just a miner injury.

It takes 5 dwarves to change a lightbulb. One to hold it and four to drink until the room spins

An elf, a human, and a teifling walk into a bar. The dwarf laughed and walked under it.

ELVES

When the forest folk need to learn new skills, they turn to elf-help books.

Drow are good philosophers. They're very deep.

When a dark elf casts sleep on you, do you get drowsy?

Not all elves are stuck up and arrogant. Some have low elf esteem

I put pointy ears on a field mouse. I'm really proud of mouse-elf.

High elves have lots of tomes. They keep them on Booksh-elfs.

Since the fae live a long time, they can accumulate a lot of treasure. They become welfy.

To learn elvish language, you first need to learn the Elf-abet

A thousand year old fae is a Millenielf.

Our town has a person dedicated to the welfare of our non-human residents. An Elf and Safety Official.

Elves have long ears, because there needs to be a point to them.

What do you call a dozen elves? Twelves.

Elves are great listeners. They're all ears.

GNOMES

Gnomish barbers are really fast. They have a lot of short cuts.

In fantasy, there are a lot of different words for little people. They have a totally different gnomenclature.

Gnome that keeps good time. Metro-gnome

Never borrow money from gnomes. They're always a little short.

What do gnomes do after school? Gnomework.

What do I know about gnomes? Very little.

HALFLINGS

Halflings are great party members, because they don't look down on people.

I've been told that the little things count, so I teach accounting to Halflings.

"It's strange how little things change," I said. The Fighter slapped me and told me to stop staring at the Halflings.

Today was so hot, two halflings came by, and threw a ring into my house.

5 MONSTERS

GENERAL MAYHEM MONSTERS

Beauty is in the eye of the Beholder. Also Sleep, Slow, and Telekinesis.

A Beholder's favorite food is Eye Scream.

What happens when you cut an ear off an Owlbear. You get an Owlb.

The party found a pack of meditating kobolds pondering the nature of the world. They were wondering monsters.

Treants aren't dangerous. They're all bark.

Treants are tough. You have to take them out whittle by whittle.

What is green, has no head, and flies. A dead orc.

Water elementals don't say hello, they just wave.

What monster dumps all their bonuses into one stat? A Min-maxotaur.

A Shambling Mound's favorite drink is Root Beer.

You can't blame Sprites for being tricksters. You're in their Nature.

A Leviathan's favorite food is fish and ships.

We were worried that there were mimics about, but the table assured us it was perfectly safe.

The barkeep asked why we carried weapons in a tavern. Mimics we said. He laughed. We laughed. The table laughed. We killed the table. Good times.

How do you keep a minotaur from charging? Take away his credit cards.

The wizard threw a book at the large bird, killing it. Paper beats Roc.

Medusa have hard time with relationships. They're always objectifying people.

Goblin bandits are Rob-Goblins.

There's a half-horse, half-man in the middle of that village. He's the centaur of attention.

They say you can put snakes in your hair to cure migraines. I find that oddly Medusinal.

Why did the specter cross the road? To get to The Other Side.

My seven headed monster was stolen! I'm dehydrated.

How do you talk to giants? Use big words.

Never make friends with a vampire. They're a pain in the neck.

I have a fear of giants. Fee-fi-phobia.

A horse that only comes out after dark is a nightmare.

Our party adopted a baby cow-kin. A Mini-taur.

Elementals are not immune to medusa petrification. In case of fire use stares.

What do you call a goblin with three eyes. Gobliiin

Medusas favorite cheese is Gorgon-zola.

DRAGONS

Dragons don't like surprise parties... of adventurers.

Some dragons are all about law and order. They're Coppers.

Dragons eat Will-o-wisps when they want a light snack.

Dragons are the worse story tellers because the drag-on.

Dragons sleep during the day because they hunt knights.

Models of dragons are not to scale.

Dragons that observe the sabbath because they only prey on weak knights.

Dragons don't poop gold. It would be a gross waste of resources.

Dragons snack on firecrackers.

What does a mama dragon say to a hatchling? Whelp

that's a good start.

Dragons are horrible bosses. Everyone gets fired.

Awake dragon, drag-on. Sleeping dragon, drag-off.

How much does a dragon weigh? depends on the scales.

Some male dragons can't reproduce. They have reptile dysfunction.

My tiny dragon is named newt, because he's my newt

Some dragons smell. What a skink.

Some color changing dragons tell jokes. They are stand up chameleons.

What do you call an observant Dragon? A monitor lizard.

Illusionary dragons are fake newts.

What do you say to a dragon red with anger? Calmer, calmer, calmer chameleon.

Dragons are downright mean. They're cold blooded.

What do you call a stoned dragon? A Mariguana.

Dragons sleep during the day to fight knights!

A dragon's favorite dessert is lair cake.

In a fight with a dragon, I grabbed it by the tail. He said, "This is the end of me."

Dragons don't make plans. They wing it.

I'm a dragon. I'm always dragon myself to work, school, and the post office.

I once met a cow that slew a dragon. She was legend-dairy.

You can always tell how much a dragon weighs by looking at the scales.

The sign said, “Beware of Dog.” Dog is a terrible name for a Dragon.

Some dragons horde books. They’re known as book wyrms.

A dragon’s favorite steak, flaming yawn.

A little known fact is that dragons are good musicians. They really know their scales.

My friend the dragon recently did her nails. She entered them in a talon show.

OGRE

What do you call an average ogre? Mediogre.

As the large heavy set man expired, he wheezed with his last breath, “My time here is ogre.”

“You’re brutish, overweight and mean,” she yelled. “This relationship is ogre.”

“Where’d you see them?” “Somewhere ogre there.”

There were more ogres than he could handle. It was an ogre dose.

The brutes came at us in waves, ogre and ogre again. It was ogre whelming.

Raiding farms, stealing cows, threatening villagers. People say I work too hard, but I've always been an ogre achiever.

Some people like Shrek. I think it's ogre rated.

The raiders are coming. It'll be all ogre soon.

People hide when I attack. They don't want to be ogre run.

SPRITES AND FAIRIES

I once knew a thoughtful spite. Thinkerbell

You can't take pictures of fairies. They get pixie-lated.

Was it a good deal with the fae? No, but it was Fairy-nuff

The opposite of sprite, spleft.

Sometime I take the R out of sprite, just for spite

Sad sprites get soda pressed

My fairy godmother asked if I wanted a long life or a long memory. I forget my response.

TROLLS

What did the troll say when he was cut in two? Thanks for halving me.

He's the head troll in charge. He's in con-troll.

How do you stop a troll? Seize their memes of production.

He was a troll that didn't do things in halves. He went the troll nine yards

Trolls have a favorite kind of music: Rock and Troll

He was a troll you could look up to. A real troll model.

He always told the truth, the troll truth, and nothing but the truth.

He'll never give you up, or set you down, turn around or desert you: Rick Troll

I'm not ready to deal with my fear of trolls. I'll cross that bridge when I come to it.

The troll guarding the stone bridge is my arch enemy.

How many trolls does it take to light a candle? One, but he's extremely careful.

UNDEAD

Zombies don't write music. They decompose.

My friend was kidnapped by undead, but he's all wight now.

Don't drink the Ghoul-Aid. It causes paralysis.

I know a necromancer who now lives alone. His Wight left him.

I used to be a Skeleton, and now I'm a Flame Skull. I could have gone further, but I decided to quit while I was a head.

If the undead is surprised, it's a ghast.

The local vampire coven wants to expand. They're looking for new blood.

There are undead bees. Zombees if you will.

Just saw two zombies on a date. And they say romance is dead.

People don't believe me when I tell them I've become a zombie, but I'm dead serious.

I once told a bad joke to a ghost. It still haunts me to this day.

Figuring out how to starve a zombie isn't difficult. It's a no-brainer.

Ghosts read a lot. They go through books quickly.

The dungeon is filled with vampire mice. Mouse-qitoes.

Ghosts are bad liars. You can see right through them.

WITCH

Witches have lovely handwriting. It's all curse-ive.

Our witch has a magic skillet. It's made of Cast Iron.

My witch friend gave up fortune telling, because there wasn't any future in it.

Witches: don't be caught without spell components. Visit Rite aid before your ritual!

Witches love their rides. It goes broom, broom!

How many witches does it take to change a lightbulb?
It depends on what you want to change it into.

VICIOUS MOCKERY INSULTS

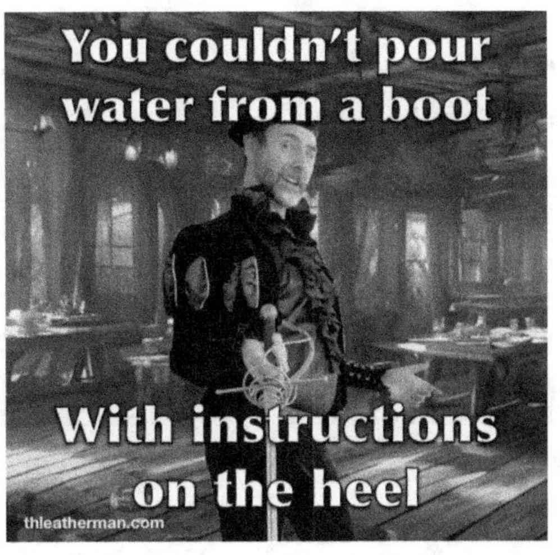

He's as sharp as a marble.

At this point, you can only impress me.

You've got two brain cells and they are fighting for third place.

You're not the biggest idiot in the kingdom, but you better hope they don't die.

It's impossible to underestimate you.

You're a coward and history will forget you.

Your mother was a hamster, and your father smelled of elderberries. (Ah, the classics)

You have a face a mother wouldn't love.

If you bathed in an outhouse, you'd smell better.

You're a leprous spot on civilization.

You've got three brain cells and four of them don't work.

I pity the Mind Flayer feasting on your brain.

Who cast Animate Dead, because you don't smell like anything living.

Are you cursed, or did you intentionally dress that way?

Is your charisma always that low or did you fall down some stairs recently?

Disguise Self can't fix that.

Are you sure you use magic, because I seriously doubt you can spell.

I see your dump stat was every stat.

I admire your dedication to keeping your weapon clean. I mean, you haven't hit me yet.

You must be a peasant, because you have no class.

If I cast Detect Thoughts on you, I'd take psychic damage.

I'm going to cast Stinking Cloud to improve your smell.

Talking to you decreased my intelligence.

You're so putrid, I wouldn't touch you with Mage Hand.

Are you part dragon, because your breath could be a weapon.

With that face, I bet you were in a tragic accident.

You're the living embodiment of Psychic Scream.

You're number 1 in my book. A critical failure.

Given how you look, I bet whatever disease you have is hard to pronounce.

I'm going to cast False Life on you, because you sure need one.

Let's finish this battle, because being a corpse will be such an improvement for you.

Tasha's Hideous Laughter, or is that really your face?

Did your parents have any children that lived?

I'm sorry. You're not worth my time.

I'm busy. Can I ignore you later?

That's a face a mother could kill.

I'd insult you, but with that face life must be hard enough for you.

Did your dad have a thing for hags?

Your mom is an amazing woman, but I wouldn’t ride her into battle.

I'd like to see things from your point of view, but I couldn't get my head as far up my butt as you can.

I'm not insulting you. I'm describing you.

You make perfect sense. It must be time for me to take my medication.

I wasn't born with enough middle fingers to show know how I feel about you.

Stupidity is not a crime, so you are free to go.

You aren't stupid. You just have a bad luck when thinking.

I don't think you act stupid. I'm sure it's the real thing.

I'm sorry I hurt your feelings when I called you stupid. I thought you already knew.

If Mind Flayers attack, don't worry. You're safe.

Your eyes are open, mouth moving, but Mr. Brain has long since departed, eh?

I've met carrots with better fighting skills than you.

Are you trying to defeat me with you smell?

If your intelligence was a Wand of Blasting, you wouldn't have enough energy to blow your nose.

Are you sure you want to fight? Most people have an aversion to embarrassing themselves in public.

You smell worse than a necromancer's workshop!

About the Author

TH Leatherman is a writer and humorist from Firestone, Colorado. He enjoys science fiction, fantasy, puns (lots of puns), winemaking, and the Rocky Mountain lifestyle. When not busy writing his next book, he can be found hiking with his wife and two sons or walking his rescued dogs. He has worked as a stockbroker, street performer, and volunteer wrangler. He graduated Summa Cum Laude from Regis University with a degree in Business Management and a minor in Psychology.

Connect with Mr. Leatherman

Check out his blog and links to other books – psst. There's also a free book if you sign up for his mailing list.

https://thleatherman.com/

More puns, jokes, and one-liners

https://www.facebook.com/TH-Leatherman

@thleatherman on Twitter

TH.Leatherman on Instagram

Reviews!

Authors (especially me) love reviews. Good, bad, or indifferent tell me what you think. You can do it easily on Amazon and Goodreads, but anywhere book lovers congregate is appreciated.

www.ingramcontent.com/pod-product-compliance
Lightning Source LLC
Chambersburg PA
CBHW071356200726
48294CB00004B/1184
* 9 7 8 1 7 3 5 3 9 9 0 9 6 *